AT THE PIANO
SCOTT JOPLIN

MW00465410

Alfred
E D I T E D   B Y
MAURICE HINSON

Illustration: Ted Engelbart

© Copyright MCMXC by Alfred Publishing Co., Inc.

AT THE PIANO
WITH
SCOTT JOPLIN
A Guide to Style and Interpretation

Edited by Maurice Hinson

CONTENTS

This edition is dedicated to
Dr. Jean Barr
with appreciation
and admiration.
Maurice Hinson

Foreword

Ragtime was very popular from roughly 1890 to 1920, and by 1900 it had swept the country. Its popularity reached its height around 1910, after which it gradually waned. However, elements of ragtime survived in jazz and other forms of American and European music. During World War II a ragtime revival occurred, and in 1973 the movie *The Sting* made famous Scott Joplin's rag "The Entertainer," which sparked another revival that continues today.

"Ragtime couldn't have happened anywhere but this country," pianist Max Morath says. "It's got everything in it because America's everybody. You have this tremendous flux, and you can see it in ragtime. You have European forms, you have West Indies and Spanish influences, you have tremendous influence from Protestant church music." Other influences include folk dances, Irish jigs and polkas. It contains some of the charm, elegance and primness of late Victorian culture, plus some of the boisterousness that characterizes the folk songs and dances of frontier America. Joplin's rags were written essentially in the romantic tradition of 19th-century piano music and contain suggestions of Chopin, Liszt and Schubert. One writer has said that Joplin's rags "are the precise American equivalent, in terms of a native style of dance music, of minuets by Mozart, mazurkas by Chopin or waltzes by Brahms."[1]

With its lighthearted gaiety, ragtime encouraged people to forget about their problems and simply have fun. Its infectious, syncopated beat made it fresh sounding, and its appeal is just as strong today as it was when it first appeared. Since 1973, ragtime has reemerged in the musical consciousness. This collection contains some of the finest rags ever composed by Scott Joplin—the leading figure in ragtime and a man very much in tune with his times—and some of his collaborators. Joplin was the best—the most professional, the most original and the most serious of all the ragtime composers. His music has finally received its proper due in American piano repertoire.

Background and Development of Ragtime

Ragtime originated in the 1830s and 1840s in slave cabins, on Mississippi River plantations, and in native dances of New Orleans. Plantation banjos and rippling drumbeats found their counterpart in the traveling minstrel shows performed by blacks or by whites made up in blackface. The minstrels were important in introducing white audiences to black music. It was the itinerant black "piano professors" in the tenderloin districts of Mississippi valley towns such as New Orleans, Memphis and St. Louis who actually developed what came to be known as ragtime. Ragtime was, one might say, basically an African-American piano version of the polka or its analog, the John Philip Sousa-style march.

The easy money floating around the poolhalls and saloons was more than enough to support the entertainers who worked there. This attracted black musicians, there being no place else for them to play. Ragtime was thus a folk music that transmitted the content and spirit of black folk/dance tunes within a colorful and aesthetically interesting framework.

In 1897 ragtime made its commercial debut with "Mississippi Rag" by William H. Krell, the first instrumental piece to be published written completely in ragtime style. By 1900 the ragtime craze was sweeping the country. In 1899 Scott Joplin's "Maple Leaf Rag" was published and eventually became the nation's first million-seller in sheet music sales.

Today ragtime is recognized as an important American contribution to music. It has influenced many 20th-century composers, including Debussy, Hindemith, Ives, Milhaud, Ravel, Satie and Stravinsky. Even the great 19th-century composer Johannes Brahms entertained the idea of a ragtime piece late in his life. Some of our outstanding contemporary American composers such as William Albright and William Bolcom incorporate ragtime influence with contemporary compositional techniques in their works.

1. H. Wiley Hitchcock. *Stereo Review* (April 1971). p. 84.

Musical Characteristics of Ragtime

Ragtime uses a pattern of repeated rhythms and a great deal of syncopation. The term "ragtime" was probably derived from the "ragged" effect produced by the syncopated melodies. A syncopated note is one that falls between two beats rather than on one or the other, so that the normally weak beat is accented. This gives a cheerful, vigorous character to the music.

*indicates the syncopated or offbeat notes
Scott Joplin, "The Entertainer," measures 5–6

In this example, Joplin used one of the most common means of creating syncopation: *offbeats*. "Offbeats" is a term that refers to notes, not beats, that have been displaced in the measure so that they do not coincide with the beats of the measure but occur between them. Beats are felt most easily when they are emphasized by notes beginning at the same time. Offbeats work against this principle. Joplin creates offbeats in the example from "The Entertainer" by having the first eighth note in measure 1 occur "too quickly." The first note of the measure, a 16th, only takes up half of the first beat, and the eighth then takes up the second half of this beat and the first half of the next. Thus when the second beat occurs, the note is still sustaining and there is no new note to emphasize this beat. A stronger offbeat occurs at the end of the measure, when the C 16th note is tied into the C quarter note beginning the second measure. There is no new note to emphasize the first beat of the second measure; it is still sustaining from measure 1, and since it is a strong downbeat, avoiding this expected accent creates a strong syncopation.

In ragtime, not all notes are syncopated, but the syncopated notes stand out, so that each right-hand phrase seems to be set in opposition to the steady, cakewalk-derived rhythm of the left hand. This "boom-chick" bass, as it has also been known, moves approximately at half the speed of the melody, and is somewhat similar to the basso continuo or continuous bass of the 18th century.

or more complicated versions such as

or

Other characteristics include duple meters (2/4 or 4/4); functional harmony that stresses tonic, dominant and subdominant; contrasted melodic/rhythmic sections with 16- or 32-measure periods and short introductions; vamps (a simple introductory or accompaniment phrase or chord progression that can be repeated indefinitely until the melody begins); and codas. Modulation is a predominant trait in ragtime. Each piece in this collection contains at least one key change, and more often than not ends in a different key than it started with. Architecturally, a rag is made up of a sequence of three, four or even five sections, one or more of which is repeated. These do not develop out of each other, but are more or less independent, much as in a march.

Scott Joplin's "School of Ragtime"

With the success of "Maple Leaf Rag," Scott Joplin was able to leave the honky-tonks, establish himself as a piano teacher, and devote more time to composing. During 1908 in New York he wrote a truly valuable document entitled *School of Ragtime*, which helped establish the basic elements of good ragtime style.

REMARKS

What is scurrilously called ragtime is an invention that is here to stay. That is now conceded by all classes of musicians. That all publications masquerading under the name of ragtime are not the genuine article will be better known when these exercises are studied. That real ragtime of the higher class is rather difficult to play is a painful truth which most pianists have discovered. Syncopations are no indication of light or trashy music, and to shy bricks at "hateful ragtime" no longer passes for musical culture. To assist amateur players in giving the "Joplin Rags" that weird and intoxicating effect intended by the composer is the object of this work.

SCHOOL OF RAGTIME
by
Scott Joplin

Exercise No. 1

It is evident that, by giving each note its proper time and by scrupulously observing the ties, you will get the effect. So many are careless in these respects that we will specify each feature. In this number, strike the first note and hold it through the time belonging to the second note. The upper staff is not syncopated, and is not to be played. The perpendicular dotted lines running from the syncopated note below to the two notes above will show exactly its duration. Play slowly until you catch the swing, and never play ragtime fast at any time.

Slow march tempo *(Count Two)*

Exercise No. 2

This style is rather more difficult, especially for those who are careless with the left hand, and are prone to vamp. The first note should be given the full length of three sixteenths, and no more. The second note is struck in its proper place and the third note is not struck but is joined with the second as though they were one note. This treatment is continued to the end of the exercise.

Slow march tempo *(Count Two)*

SCHOOL OF RAGTIME
by
Scott Joplin
(continued)

Exercise No. 3

This style is very effective when neatly played. If you have observed the object of the dotted lines they will lead you to a proper rendering of this number and you will find it interesting.

Slow march tempo *(Count Two)*

Exercise No. 4

The fourth and fifth notes here form one tone, and also in the middle of the second measure and so to the end. You will observe that it is a syncopation only when the tied notes are on the same degree of the staff. Slurs indicate a legato movement.

Slow march tempo *(Count Two)*

Exercise No. 5

The first ragtime effect here is the second note, right hand, but, instead of a tie, it is an eighth note: rather than two sixteenths with tie. In the last part of this measure, the tie is used because the tone is carried across the bar. This is a pretty style and not as difficult as it seems on first trial.

Slow march tempo *(Count Two)*

Exercise No. 6

The instructions given, together with the dotted lines, will enable you to interpret this variety which has very pleasing effects. We wish to say here, that the "Joplin ragtime" is destroyed by careless or imperfect rendering, and very often good players lose the effect entirely, by playing too fast. They are harmonized with the supposition that each note will be played as it is written, as it takes this and also the proper time divisions to complete the sense intended.

Slow march tempo *(Count Two)*

Interpreting Ragtime

The piano was the principal instrument of ragtime. The ragtime pianist's touch was somewhat percussive and the damper pedal not often used. Rags should be performed in a fairly strict, moderate tempo and the syncopations played in precise 16th notes. "Slow march time" (♩ = ca. 100) seems to be the description of what early rag scores playfully indicated as "Tempo di Rag." Tempo changes and free rubato usage are foreign to ragtime style. The eighth notes of the melody should be played "straight," not unevenly, as is usual in jazz, and the pianist should aim for a cantabile melodic line, even with strong rhythms or sharp accents in the left-hand part. Joplin always played extremely cantabile (i.e., in a singing style). This cannot be emphasized strongly enough.

Dynamic and pedal marks are rare in the original scores, and ragtime must not be overpedaled. In general, pedal should not be used to sustain the bass notes played on the first and third eighths; this will allow the offbeat to be crisply accented. The player should aim for the good phrasing characteristic of all fine keyboard performance.

These guidelines may be altered to suit the performer, for the pianists of the ragtime era were anxious to develop their own personal styles. The one rule that Joplin constantly reminded the pianist to observe was: "Do not play this piece fast. It is never right to play Ragtime fast." But the pianist should remember that any piece of music dictates—within fairly clear limits—its own proper tempo. Joplin's rule must be understood as being relative to his time, when many "speed" players were ruining the rags by displaying only their digital velocity. So Joplin's "not fast" instruction was probably relative to the destructive prestissimos of his day. It also seems apparent from Joplin's repeated instructions to play his music slowly and correctly, that he was concerned that it be treated with care and dignity, that he envisioned performances as "classical," as elegant and faithful to his notation.

The published score is only one performance possibility. Certainly on repeats the pianist may elaborate or simplify the text, so long as the melodic line and original harmonies are not changed. We know from his recordings that Joplin varied repeated sections. A piano roll Joplin made in 1914 of his "Magnetic Rag" shows that he used short passages of "walking bass" in repeats not found in the score. Octave passages may be replaced by single notes, according to the ability of the pianist. The melody could be played an octave higher on the repeat to highlight treble brilliance.

Joplin used two characteristic dynamic indications in some of the rags, *f-p* and *p-f*. An *f-p* means that the section is to be played forte the first time and piano the second; *p-f* indicates the reverse.

Since Joplin strived for a "classical" excellence in his music and recognition as a composer of artistic merit, he and his publisher John Stark referred to his pieces as "classic rags." "Classic" ragtime is a highly formal, graceful, sometimes delicate and deliberate music that has more in common with the baroque period than with the late 19th-century cabaret where it was, in part, developed. Within its framework there is a wealth of music.

Ragtime is an art that deserves the same serious study given to Bach, Chopin or Debussy. It requires imagination, skill and taste for an authentic performance.

About This Collection

At the Piano with Scott Joplin is a performing edition aimed at helping the pianist perform ragtime music in a stylistically appropriate manner. All fingering, pedaling and metronome marks are editorial unless stated otherwise. Dynamics, unless placed in parentheses, are Scott Joplin's original indications. The pieces in this collection are organized alphabetically by title. All of the pieces involve Scott Joplin, the greatest writer of rags, either as composer or as composer-collaborator. The rags range in difficulty from intermediate to moderately difficult. All of the rags in this collection are based on first editions, which are identified in the following section.

About the Music

This rag is program music that received its name from the Cascade Gardens of the 1904 St. Louis World's Fair. This interesting watercourse of cascades, fountains and lagoons was a central feature of the fair. Joplin's delightful piece also flows and ripples while building an infectious swing. All repeated sections should feature the right hand played one octave higher. The first theme has an ascending arpeggio (measures 11–12) similar to the one in "Maple Leaf Rag" (measures 7–8), but here in sixths. The fourth theme (measure 57 to the end) is based harmonically on "Maple Leaf," while the trio (measures 41–56) develops a "stride" bass that frequently introduces thundering octaves. This rag shows that Joplin, while retaining the vigor of black folk elements, was also continually refining his material. It is one of the pinnacles of classic ragtime.

Source: First edition, John Stark & Son, St. Louis, 1904.

The Chrysanthemum
This rag contains a tantalizing and whirling pattern à la bourrée in measures 21–36. The trio (measures 53–68, and 85 to the end) is especially personal, and is filled with a gently syncopated rhythm that Joplin marks piano and dolce. Yet this mood still retains the swing quality essential to the style. The entire rag is a lacework of sound, with every nook and cranny filled with lyrical embroidery. Stark, Joplin's publisher, advertised that Joplin composed this piece as a result of a dream he had after reading *Alice's Adventures in Wonderland*, and the fantasy aura about it lends support to this assertion. Joplin was very careful in marking the pedal and dynamics. This edition uses only his indications in these areas. Be sure to use a good legato touch throughout the trio.

Source: First edition, John Stark & Son, St. Louis, 1904.

This jaunty piece was the first publication of one of Joplin's own works and is one of the favorite pieces from his early period. A captivatingly melodious rag, it should move at a very comfortable tempo so that the beauty of the music can be exposed. The left-hand octaves at measures 12, 44, 56, 57, 59, 60, 61, 65, 67, 76, 80, 82 and 84 should be slightly accented. This is the rag that was used in the 1973 movie *The Sting* and helped spark a revival of ragtime.

Source: First edition, Joplin in St. Louis, 1901.

This rag contains some beguiling melodies that are as sunny as any that Joplin ever composed; their frank, open, folklike qualities artfully conceal a fastidious art. It was dedicated to James Brown and his Mandolin Club, and some of its melodies do recall the pluckings and fast tremolos of this once- popular instrument. Monroe H. Rosenfeld, writing in the June 7, 1903, issue of the St. Louis *Globe-Democrat*, said of this piece: "It is a jingling work of a very original character, embracing various strains of a retentive character which set the foot in spontaneous action and leave an indelible imprint on the tympanum." The numerous crescendos and few decrescendos add much interest and must be carefully observed. Be sure to repeat measures 21–36 one octave higher and at a quieter dynamic level than the first time through.

Source: First edition, John Stark & Son, St. Louis, 1902.

Heliotrope Bouquet—A Slow Drag Two-Step
This rag was composed in conjunction with Louis Chauvin (1882–1907). Chauvin was a gifted Creole—part Ibo, part Indian and part French—who played in clubs in Chicago. He contributed the first two themes and Joplin contributed the rest. The atmosphere of Chauvin's themes seems to have suggested the title, and its exquisite harmony helps make it one of the masterpieces of ragtime literature. Its rhythms contain a Spanish tinge. John Stark, the original publisher, advertised it as "the audible poetry of motion," and its lilting, graceful flow supports that advertisement. There is a serenity in many of Joplin's rags that is reflected in his flower titles—"The Chrysanthemum," "Heliotrope Bouquet," "Sun Flower Slow Drag"—and in other titles such as "Euphonic Sounds." Measures 5–52 (Chauvin's themes) require more legato and pedal than most rags. Joplin even marks legato at measure 53 (the beginning of his material) to continue Chauvin's atmosphere.

Source: First edition, Stark Music Printing and Publishing Co., New York and St. Louis, 1907.

This was Joplin's second published rag, and it swept the country in 1899 as a nationwide hit. It remains the most famous of all rags. John Stark, the publisher, purchased "Maple Leaf Rag" for fifty dollars with an arrangement for continuing royalty to Joplin. This early rag contains strong rhythmic elements built from reiterated syncopations, plus lilting tunes developed from the cakewalk. Its four themes (**ABACD**; each letter represents a 16-measure section) must ripple out over the striding bass. This rag indicated the direction Joplin would take in these pieces: the opening theme captured the ear and imagination; then each succeeding theme formed an episode in the musical story. The final theme then had the last word, or wrapped up the story. In April 1916 Joplin recorded several rolls for the Connorized label, and this smooth performance showed that Joplin made a few additions (for example, extra fill-in octaves in the left hand) on the repeated sections. Our edition shows those additions in cue-size notes. Joplin also played measures 17–24, 49–58 and 65–80 one octave higher on the repeat. Composer Charles Griffes had much respect for this rag and played it often at private gatherings.

Source: First edition, John Stark & Co., Sedalia, 1899.

This rag is a condensed version of an earlier 1899 failed piece of the same name that was a sort of ragtime ballet based on Negro social dances of the time, with sung narration. The 1906 rag was an attempt to recoup the losses of the earlier version. This piece introduced a novel performance practice called "stop time." To produce this effect, the pianist should stamp the heel of one foot heavily upon the floor when the word "stamp" is indicated. The toe is not to be raised from the floor while stamping. Some of the "stamps" occur during rests in the music, and this frequently encourages the audience to clap during the "stop-time" sections. Vary dynamics during the repeated sections.

Source: First edition, the Stark Music Co., St. Louis and New York, 1906.

This is Joplin's only work in tango rhythm. Originally from Africa, where it was known by its tribal name, *tangana*, and then by way of Cuba, this rhythm was heard as early as 1860 in the piano piece "Souvenir de la Havane" by the American composer Louis Moreau Gottschalk (1829–1869). The swooping slides in measures 21–26 must be played smoothly. Joplin indicated the pedal marks in this section. This piece is superb throughout and represents Joplin at his best.

Source: First edition, Seminary Music Co., New York, 1909.

This bouncy rag has introductions to the **A** and **C** sections. Its form is **ABACD**. It requires a good octave technique in both hands. In the **D** section repeat, the inner thirds and/or sixths can be dropped from the right-hand octaves, thereby making this section a little easier. The piano indication at the beginning of the **C** section (measure 57) should be carefully observed the first time through. For the repeat, play the right hand one octave higher and increase the dynamic level to forte.

Source: First edition, John Stark & Son, St. Louis, 1902.

This is one of the early gems of ragtime. Joplin demonstrates great musical rapport here with his friend Scott Hayden. John Stark wrote the advertisement for this rag and completely ignored Hayden:

> This piece came to light during the high temperature of Scott Joplin's courtship, and while he was touching the ground only in the highest places, his geese were all swans, and the Mississippi water tasted like honey-dew. ...If there ever was a song without words, this is that article: hold your ear to the ground while someone plays it, and you can hear Scott Joplin's heart beat.[2]

But this rag did help launch Hayden's career. Separate practice of the left hand in measures 7–8, 18–20 and 54–56 will be of special value. Keep measures 57–72 piano the first time through, then change to a forte on the repeat. These measures are more songlike than the rest of this dancelike rag.

Source: First edition, John Stark & Sons, St. Louis, 1901.

---

2. Rudi Blesh and Harriett Janis. *They All Played Ragtime*, p. 53. 4th ed. New York: Oak Publications, 1971.

    Joplin collaborated with his Sedalia friend on this rag. Arthur was a college classmate at the George R. Smith College for Negroes operated by the Methodist Church in Sedalia. Joplin helped him arrange and write out the material. This is the first true *slow* drag, as the instruction on the first page indicates. John Stark "designed his own cover for this composition, ...[which] depicts a small Negro boy. ...According to legend Stark discovered the little newsboy squabbling out in front of his office one day, was taken with him, and decided to bring him in and have him photographed for the cover of the new composition. Looking at the photograph, Stark decided the boy's shy expression was that of a child who had just been into the cookie jar. 'Let's call it Swipesy,' Stark said, and thus was the title of the composition born. Many rag titles came about in just such a casual manner."[3] The cakewalk is a subgenre of ragtime and American marching band repertoires. This dance originated among plantation slaves in the 1840s as a strutting promenade mocking the Southern white owners' courtly manners. Probably the most classic example appears in Claude Debussy's "Golliwog's Cakewalk." "Swipesy," an energetic rag, has all the rhythmic characteristics of the dance. Keep the tempo deliberate and slow so all the syncopations have time to be heard.

    Source: First edition, John Stark & Son, St. Louis, 1900.

For Further Reading

    Brooke Baldwin. "The Cakewalk: A Study in Stereotype and Reality." *Journal of Social History* 15 (1981):205–18.

    Edward A. Berlin. *Ragtime.* Berkeley and Los Angeles: University of California Press, 1980.

    Rudi Blesh and Harriett Janis. *They All Played Ragtime*, 4th ed. New York: Oak Publications, 1971.

    William Schafer and Johannes Riedel. *The Art of Ragtime.* Baton Rouge, LA: Louisiana State University Press, 1973.

---

3. James Haskins with Kathleen Benson. *Scott Joplin*, p. 110. Garden City, New York: Doubleday, 1978.

The Cascades
A Rag

SCOTT JOPLIN

*All pedal marks are Joplin's.

The Chrysanthemum

An Afro-American Intermezzo

Slow march tempo (♩ = c. 66)

SCOTT JOPLIN

*All pedal marks are Joplin's.

The Easy Winners

A Ragtime Two-Step

Not fast (♩ = c. 72)

SCOTT JOPLIN

*All dynamics are editorial.

22

*The fingering in measures 33-34 is Joplin's.

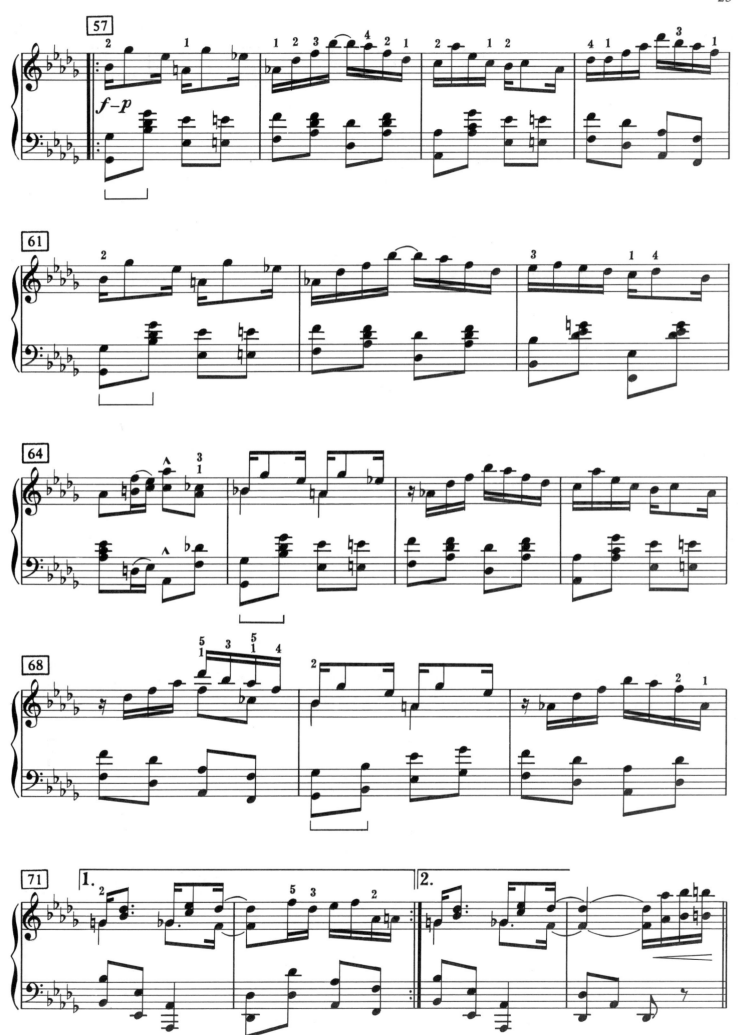

Dedicated to James Brown and his Mandolin Club

The Entertainer
A Ragtime Two-Step

SCOTT JOPLIN

Heliotrope Bouquet

A Slow Drag Two-Step

SCOTT JOPLIN
and LOUIS CHAUVIN

Slow march tempo (♩ = c. 66)

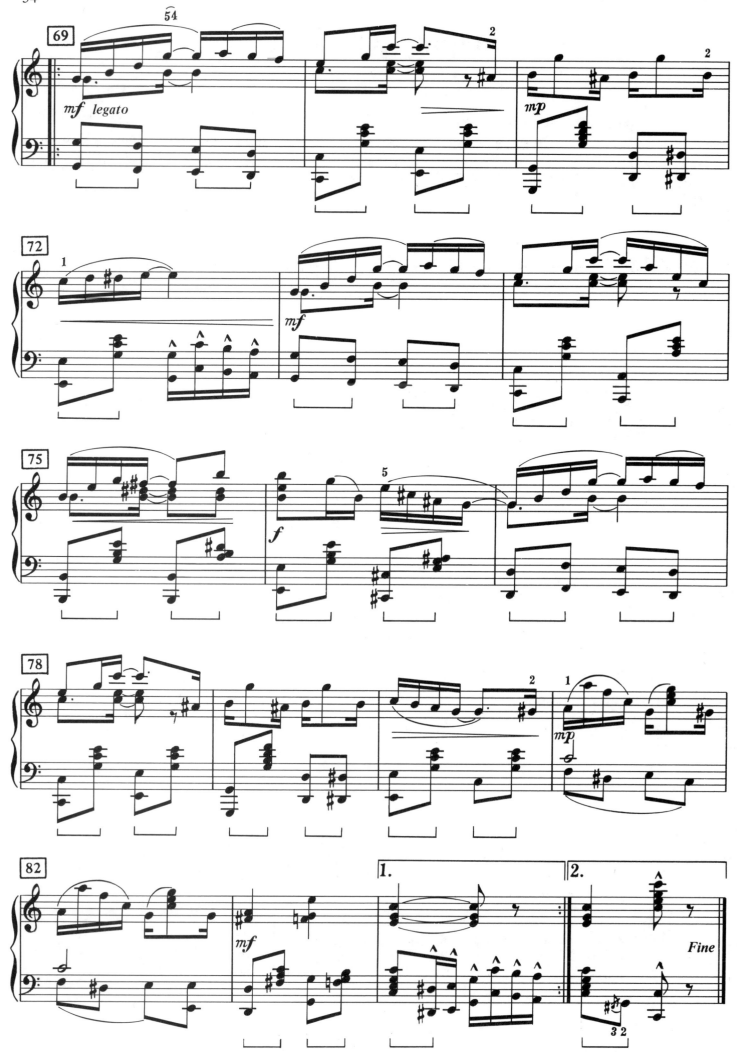

Maple Leaf Rag

SCOTT JOPLIN

(a) Joplin's tempo on his recorded piano roll is ♩ = 96

(b) All cue-size notes in this piece are the embellishments Joplin played on repeats in his piano roll of this rag.

ⓒ On repeat.

Rag-Time Dance

A Stop-Time Two-Step

SCOTT JOPLIN

NOTICE: To get the desired effect of "Stop Time" the pianist will please **Stamp** the heel of one foot heavily upon the floor at the word "Stamp". Do not raise the toe from the floor while stamping.

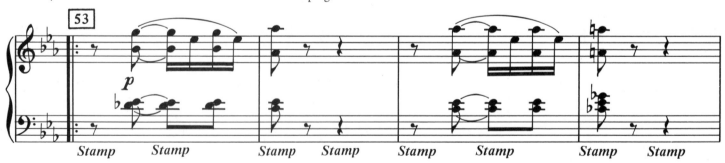

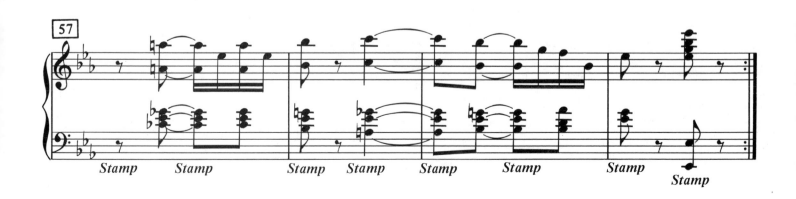

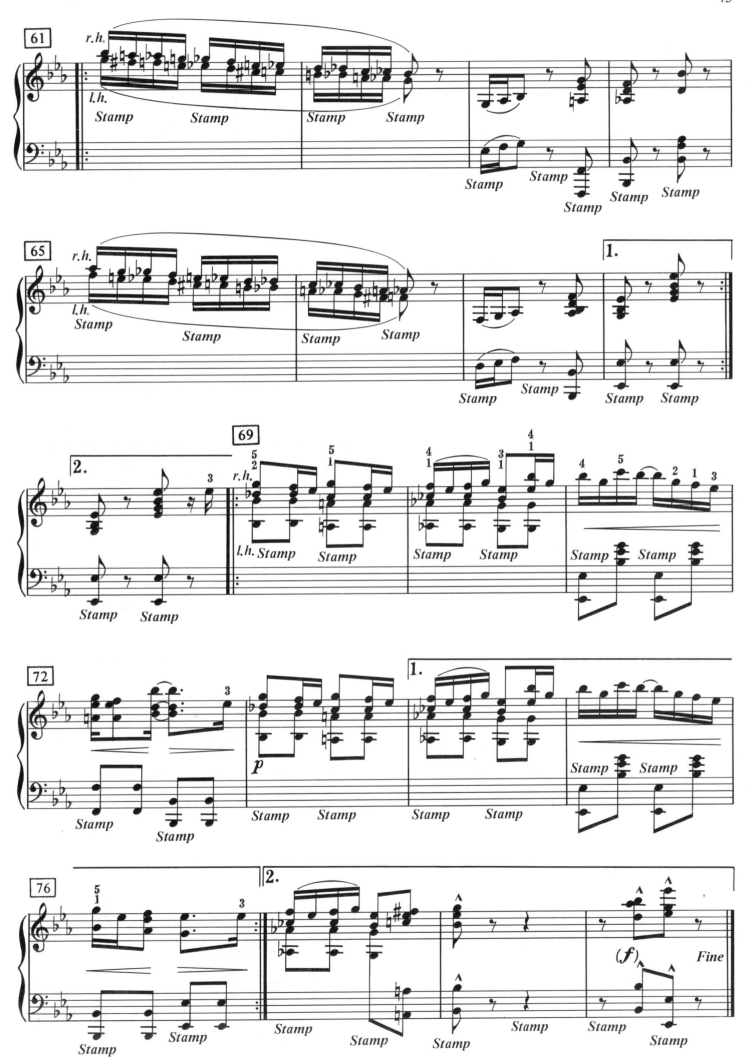

Solace
A Mexican Serenade

Very slow march time (♩ = c. 63)

SCOTT JOPLIN

*Pedal marks in measures 21-35 are Joplin's.

The Strenuous Life
A Ragtime Two-Step

Not fast (♩ = c. 72)

SCOTT JOPLIN

Sun Flower Slow Drag

Ragtime Two-Step

SCOTT JOPLIN
and SCOTT HAYDEN

Intro.
Not fast (♩ = c. 72)

Swipesy

Cakewalk

SCOTT JOPLIN
and
ARTHUR MARSHALL

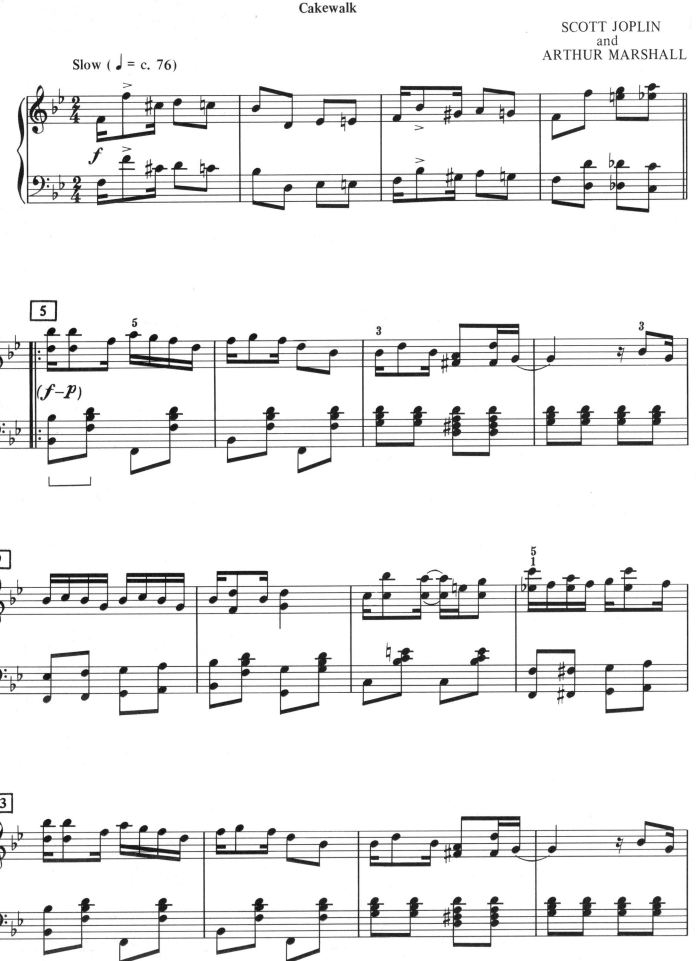

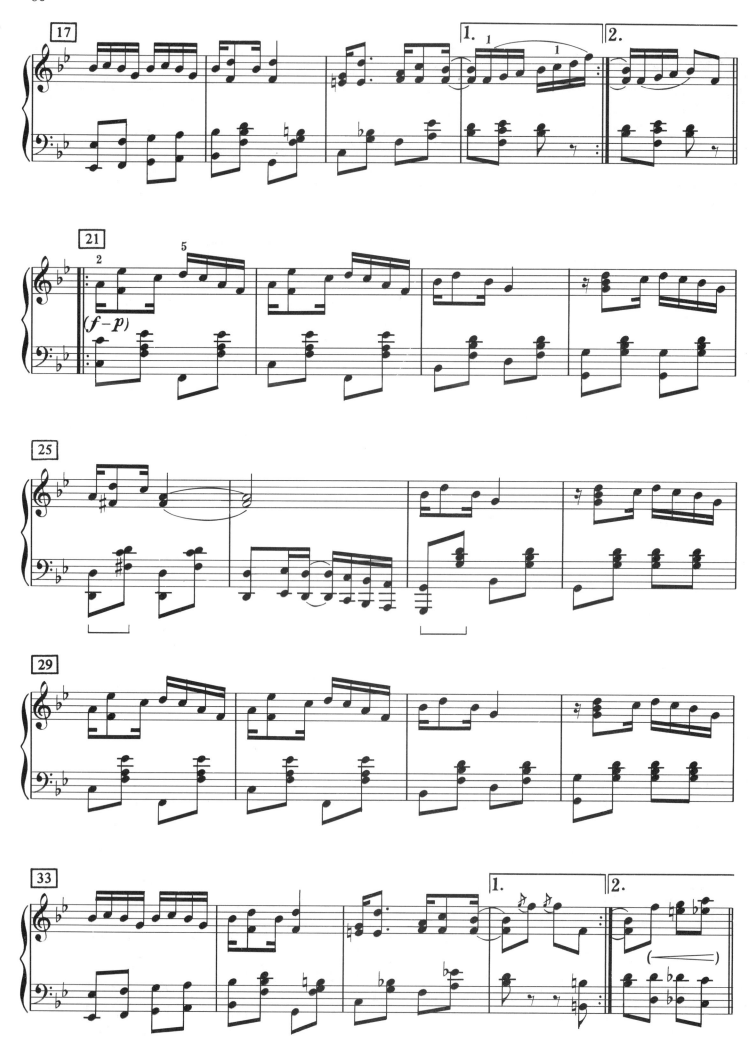